Mookie
and
The Candy Store

Love,
Mookie

+

Judith Kristen (signature)

Written by Mookie San West
Typed by Judith Kristen
Illustrated by Sue V. Daly

First published by Aquinas & Krone Publishing, LLC 1/16/2010.

ISBN # 978-0-9843526-1-6

Printed in the United States of America.

This book is printed on acid-free paper.

Cover illustration by Sue V. Daly.

Please feel welcome to visit www.illustrationsbySueDaly.com & JudithKristen.com

AND…Mookie wants all of his readers to know that the mice in this book are just figments of his glorious imagination. ...But aren't they cute?

Sue V. Daly's photo taken by Shauna L. Daly.
Image editing by Jonathan Reed West and Tim Litostansky.
Cover design by Tim Litostansky.

This book is dedicated to:
Aunt Charlotte's Candies, its dedicated employees and patrons, the wonderful Oakford family, and chocolate lovers everywhere.

Hi! It's me, Mookie! I know you kids just LOVE candy stores! Well, I love them too – but for a different reason.

Now please turn the page...have I got a sweet story for you!

As you know, I'm supposed to be a house cat. But, as hard as Mom and Dad, the other cats, and Henley try, I still manage to find my way into the great outdoors. I guess being born on a farm gave me that sense of adventure. See the rooster and the chicken? See the cows and the sheep?

They were my friends when I was a kitten. How cool is that?!

Speaking of adventure – one day as Mom opened the door for Henley to go out into the backyard, I ran out behind the old sheepdog so fast that Mom didn't even see me leave the house!

After I zipped out the backdoor, I sat by the gate for a second deciding if I should hop over it or try to squeeze through it. Just as I chose the option to leap over the gate, Henley put his paw on my tail.

"And where do you think you're goin', Adventure Boy?"

"Oh, come on, Hen…you know I'm not meant to stay in the house. I need my freedom!"

Henley sighed. "So, where to this time?"

"I don't know. Got any suggestions?"

"Have you ever been to Merchantville?" he asked me.

"Merchantville?"

"It's on the other side of Cove Road."

"No," I answered. "I always go the other way, you know, toward Meadowbrook."

"Well, you'd like it there," Henley continued, "pretty houses, cute little stores, and lots of wonderful smells coming from the pizza parlor and the diner."

"And then…there's Aunt Charlotte's!" Henley smiled.

"We have an Aunt named Charlotte who lives in Merchantville?"

"No, we don't. That's the name of the candy store."

"Henley, cats don't eat candy!"

"Maybe not, but it's a pretty cool place over there. Hey, I even have a jar filled with dog treats inside the store just waiting for me."

"No, you don't!"

"Oh, yes I do!"

"Well, Hen, there's a new adventure waiting for me out there somewhere. Please get off my tail. I gotta get going!"

"Okay. But just remember to look both ways before you cross the street!"

"I always do, Henley!"

With one good leap I was over the gate and padding my way down our driveway. Freedom, sweet freedom!

WOO-HOO!

As I started to walk up the street I saw one of my dog friends. Sheba is a sweet old gal. I like her a lot.

"Hi! Mookie! Out for a stroll?" She smiled.

"Yup. Just checkin' out the neighborhood."

"Well, have fun! And be safe!"

"I will. You too, my friend!"

I kept on strolling along and as I turned the corner another dog friend of mine called out to say hello.

"Hey there, Mook! How's it going?"

"It's goin' great!" I smiled.

This dog's name was Kahlua. Kahlua was a handsome fella and he was always very nice to me. I remember hearing someone call him a chocolate Lab. "Hmmm, I thought…chocolate."

Then I came to Cove Road. It wasn't a very wide road, but it was a busy one. I looked to the right and then to the left. I watched a few cars and trucks ride by and then I looked to the right and then to the left once again. THEN it was finally safe to cross the street.

Wow! This really is a nice place over here – just like Henley said. What a beautiful house! I like Merchantville already!

And look at the cute little stores! Can't you just smell the pizza parlor and the diner? I can! Yummy, yummy, yummy!!!

Then I walked across Park Avenue and watched a policeman as he directed traffic. "Hey there, little guy…why don't you head back to the diner? I bet Mike would give you a nice piece of fish if you knock on the back door."

I meowed and started walking up the street once again.

Then he added, "There's nothin' else up that way but Aunt Charlotte's! And cats don't eat candy!"

"Aunt Charlotte's? That's the second time I've heard that name today. Where is this place?"

No sooner had that thought left my head when I turned into a small driveway and saw a big sign right in front of me that read:

"WOW! So this is what Henley was talking about!"

The huge window below me was filled with all kinds of goodies: lots of candy, giant taffies, sparkly ribbons, pretty lace hearts, stuffed animals, balloons, and twinkling lights. This was more than a candy store.

This was **Mookie-land!**

At that very moment there was a lady locking up the store for the day. Here was my chance for adventure! Just as fast as I ran in-between Mom and Henley about an hour earlier, I ran as quick as a jackrabbit right inside the store. The lady never even saw me. The key clicked in the lock and then she was gone. And there I was inside a beautiful candy store! All by myself!

WOO-HOO!!!

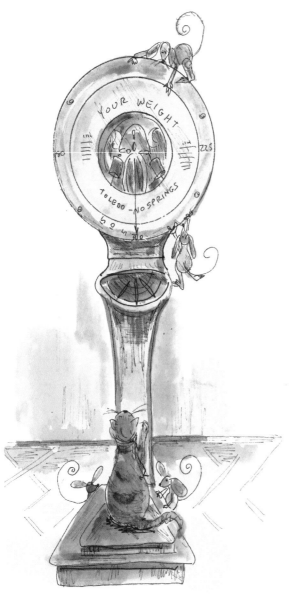

To the left of the entry was a giant brass scale. I stepped onto it. "Eight pounds! Gee, I gained a whole pound since I went to the Vet! I better lighten up on the cat treats."

I hopped off the scale and then jumped up onto a large table. Suddenly my tail puffed up like a feather duster, and I let out a big MEOW!!! YIKES!!!!! There, right next to me, was a HUGE, fuzzy, brown bear! Then I realized it was just a HUGE, fuzzy, stuffed animal and I started to relax. "Gee, they sure do make these things look real nowadays! Don't they?"

Then I hopped up onto another pretty oak table. I was immediately surrounded by: three stuffed beagles, some stuffed Teddy bears, and an orange and white tabby cat!

"Have we met before?" I smiled.

Next, I looked inside all the beautiful glass cabinets. They were filled with colorful treats: rock candy, golden chocolate coins, green spearmint leaves, gummi bears, and big red taffies. WOW! No wonder people like candy!

Across from the taffy counter was another giant tabletop that had about a thousand boxes of chocolate on it. As I said before, cats aren't candy eaters, but still, it sure looked good to me.

Then I noticed a doorway and I just had to see what was going on in there. As I walked in, directly to my right, was another wooden table filled with rolls and rolls of all kinds of colored ribbon and string: red, blue, purple, silver, yellow, green, and pink. I played around with the string and got tangled up a bit, but it sure was fun!

As I turned to see what was on the shelves nearby I spied a big glass jar on the table. It said, **Treats for Henley**. "Well, I'll be!" I laughed to myself. "Henley really does have treats here!"

Then I scampered toward an open door. More candy store fun!

I flew through the door and ran up a chocolate-colored staircase. I entered a GIANT room filled with all kinds of machines that smelled like chocolate.

I hopped onto a cart and it started to move. I drove by boxes labled: truffles, almond bark, chocolate-covered peanuts, even chocolate-covered potato chips!

I ran down the steps, walked behind the counter, and saw huge rolls of wrapping paper in lots of different colors. I liked the one with the hearts best.

Then I noticed there was a spiral staircase that was filled with all kinds of stuffed animals. "Wow! They sure do look real!" I looked into the eyes of a Mookie-sized sheepdog and said, "You aren't related to Henley by any chance, are you?"

I didn't get an answer, so, I guess that meant — No.

My adventure day was catching up with me, so I decided it was time to take a catnap. There were a few stuffed kitties already in the window, on a nice, soft bed, so I felt right at home.

Before I knew it I heard the voice of a little girl. "Mommy! Look! That's a real cat in the window!"

I didn't move an inch.

"No, Sweetheart," her mother said, "that's only a stuffed animal. They sure make them look real nowadays. Don't they?"

Then I heard a key turn in the lock and realized that those two voices belonged to the woman who opens the store, and her daughter. I had slept the whole night in the front window!

As soon as I heard the door open, I bolted from the bed and ran out of Aunt Charlotte's, down Park Avenue and across Cove Road – after looking both ways, of course.

Then I ran straight down my street, up our front walk, and meowed REAL LOUD to get back into the house. Home sweet home – at last!

"It's Mookie!" Dad opened the door and handed me to
Mom. "See, here's your boy. I told you he'd be alright."

Mom turned toward my dad and said, "Andrew? This may
sound crazy, but Mookie smells like chocolate!"

Dad leaned in toward me and agreed. "He does smell like
chocolate. A lot of chocolate! Now how did **that** happen?!"

Just then I saw Henley and Holly enter the room.

"Go on, tell them how it happened," I said to my big shaggy friend, "after all...**Mookie-land** was your idea!"

"I guess it was," he smiled at me.

"Hen?" Holly asked, "What's **Mookie-land**?!"

"Well, it's a long story, Miss Holly. Isn't it, Mookie?"

"Yup," I smiled back at Henley, "a long **sweet** story."

The End

... for now

Mookie really enjoys his life as "The Adventure Cat!"
And…his little trips around town are quite well known.
Maybe you'll even see him one of these days!
Now wouldn't THAT be sweet?!

Sue V. Daly is an award-winning illustrator specializing in pen and ink drawings. She graduated from the University of Pennsylvania, Kutztown, with a degree in Advertising Art. Sue has two daughters, Lauren and Shauna. She now lives outside Chicago with her husband Bill and her two adorable beagles, Corky and Dude. Sue is also the proud grandmom of darling twins, Emma and Andrew.

LaVergne, TN USA
14 April 2010
178901LV00002B